# THE
# LOATHSOME DRAGON

RETOLD BY DAVID WIESNER AND KIM KAHNG

WITH ILLUSTRATIONS BY

DAVID WIESNER

G. P. PUTNAM'S SONS

NEW YORK

Text copyright © 1987 by David Wiesner and Kim Kahng
Illustrations copyright © 1987 by David Wiesner
All rights reserved. Published simultaneously in
Canada by General Publishing Co. Limited, Toronto.
Printed in Hong Kong by South China Printing Co.
Book design by Nanette Stevenson    First Impression

Library of Congress Cataloging-in-Publication Data
Wiesner, David.    The loathsome dragon.
Summary: A wicked queen casts a spell over her
beautiful stepdaughter, turning her into a loathsome
dragon until such time as her wandering brother
shall return and kiss her three times.
[1. Fairy tales. 2. Folklore—England. 3. Dragons—Folklore]
I. Kahng, Kim.   II. Title
PZ8.W6335Lo   1987   398.2'1'0942   [E]   87-6964
ISBN 0-399-21407-0

*To*
*Julia and George Wiesner*

In Bamborough Castle there lived a King and Queen who had two children, a son named Childe Wynd and a daughter named Margaret. Both children were as fair as a summer's morning and were admired not only for their beauty but for their bravery as well. In time, Childe Wynd went forth to travel the world, and soon after he had gone, his mother, the Queen, died. The King mourned his wife deeply and for a long time lived alone, with only his sorrow and his daughter Margaret for company. One day while he was away hunting, he chanced to meet a magnificently beautiful enchantress. He fell instantly in love and sent word that he was bringing a new queen to Bamborough Castle.

Princess Margaret was startled to hear that she would soon have a new mother, but she was pleased that her father should be so happy. On the appointed day, she greeted the King and his new Queen at the gate with the keys to the castle in her hands. Princess Margaret bowed low and said sweetly, "Oh, welcome, Father dear, to your halls and bowers. And welcome to you, my new Mother. All that is here is yours." And she held out the keys to the castle to the new Queen.

So graceful and beautiful was Margaret that a Knight of the escort murmured admiringly, "Surely this Princess is the loveliest of her kind."

The Queen flushed with jealousy and snapped, "You would do well to remember who is now the mistress of this castle!" And to herself she muttered, "We'll see just how lovely this child can be."

That very same night, the Queen stole soundlessly down to the castle's lonely dungeon, and there in the deep darkness she did her magic. Nine times nine she passed her arms in front of herself, and three times three she chanted her magic spells. Into the darkness she whispered:

> *I will you to be a Loathsome Dragon*
> *And returned you never shall be*
> *Until Childe Wynd, the King's own son,*
> *Comes to the Heugh and thrice kisses thee.*

And so it came to be that although Margaret went to sleep a fair princess, she awoke the next morning a Loathsome Dragon.

The Dragon slithered from its bed and crawled out of the castle. It wended its way to a giant rock, called the Spindlestone Heugh, around which it coiled itself.

And soon the country round about had reason to know of the Loathsome Dragon of Spindlestone Heugh, for hunger drove the monster from its resting place to wander the kingdom, devouring all in its path.

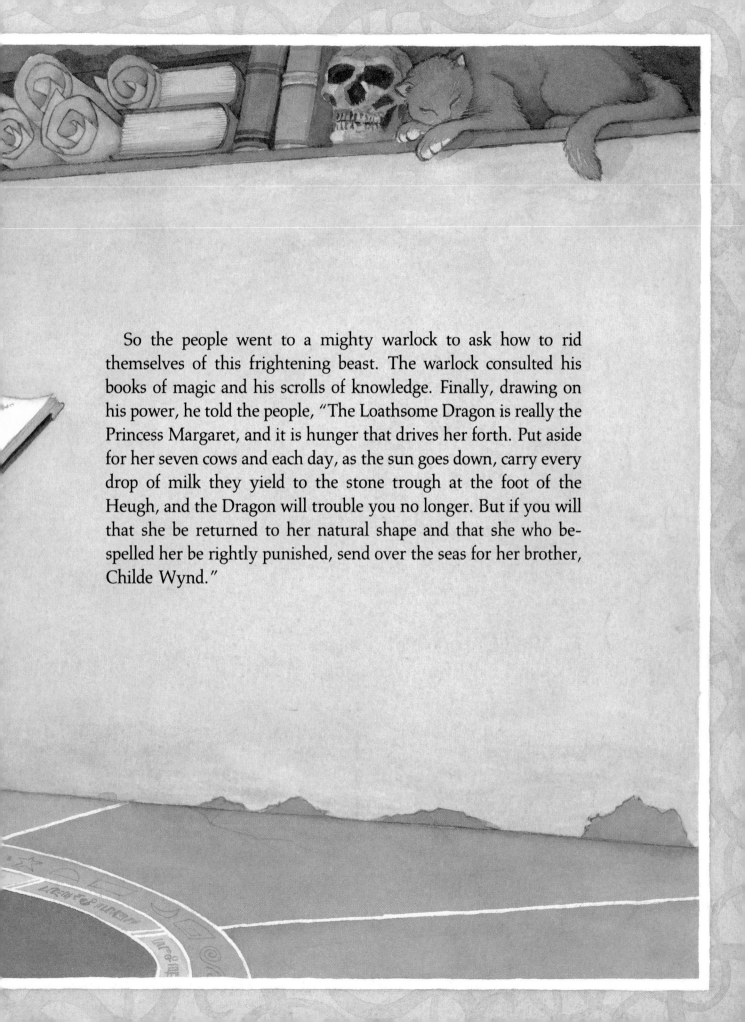

So the people went to a mighty warlock to ask how to rid themselves of this frightening beast. The warlock consulted his books of magic and his scrolls of knowledge. Finally, drawing on his power, he told the people, "The Loathsome Dragon is really the Princess Margaret, and it is hunger that drives her forth. Put aside for her seven cows and each day, as the sun goes down, carry every drop of milk they yield to the stone trough at the foot of the Heugh, and the Dragon will trouble you no longer. But if you will that she be returned to her natural shape and that she who be-spelled her be rightly punished, send over the seas for her brother, Childe Wynd."

All was done as the warlock advised; the Loathsome Dragon lived on the milk of seven cows, and the country was troubled no longer.

When Childe Wynd received word of his sister's fate, he swore a mighty oath that he would not rest until he had rescued his sister and had taken vengeance on the witch who had cast the spell. Three and thirty of his men took the oath with him. They built a great ship with a keel made of the magical rowan tree, and when all was ready, they set sail for Bamborough Castle.

Now when the Queen learned of Childe Wynd's approach, she summoned her magical wraiths and commanded, "Raise storms or bore the hull to sink his ship. Childe Wynd must never touch shore." But the ship's keel made of the rowan tree protected it against the Queen's power. "Ah . . . so Childe Wynd comes prepared," the Queen thought scornfully. "Let's see how well he can fight his own sister!" Nine times nine she passed her arms in front of herself, and three times three she chanted her magic spells, and when she had finished she had cast a new spell: So long as Childe Wynd was on the sea, the Loathsome Dragon would wait by the entrance of the harbor and keep him from the land.

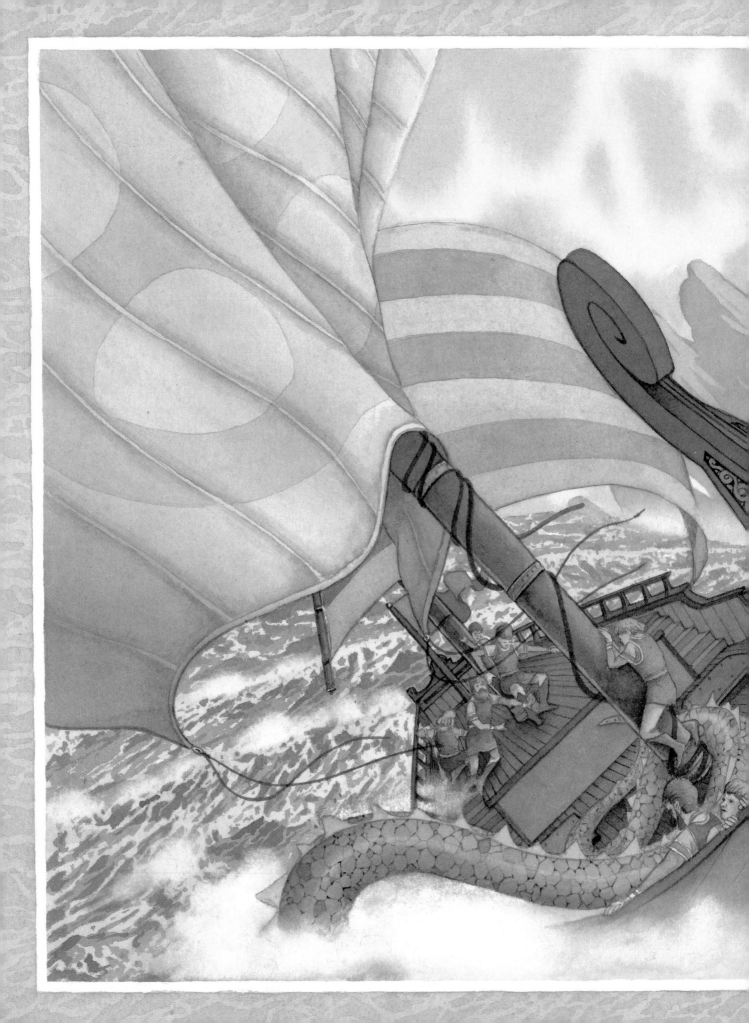

The Dragon slipped into the sea and ensnared the ship within its coils and thus held it off shore. Childe Wynd thought, "This Dragon cannot be Margaret, for she would never oppose me so." Three times Childe Wynd attempted to land, urging his men to row bravely and strongly, but each time he encountered the Loathsome Dragon. Finally Childe Wynd ordered the ship to put about. The Queen laughed triumphantly. "So much for the brave and fearless Childe Wynd. Margaret shall remain the Loathsome Dragon forever!"

Childe Wynd, however, had not truly retreated, but had only rounded the next point to land safe and unseen at Budle Creek. Seeing the Loathsome Dragon perched atop Spindlestone Heugh, he rushed forth, sword in hand. The Loathsome Dragon watched him advance and yet did nothing. Still not believing the beast could be Margaret, Childe Wynd was about to thrust his sword into the Dragon's scaly side, when the voice of his sister came from the Dragon's jaws saying:

Oh, quit your sword, forget your fear,
And give me kisses three;
For though I am a poisonous beast,
No harm I'll do to thee.

Childe Wynd stayed his hand, not knowing what to think. Was there some witchery in it or not? Again the Loathsome Dragon beseeched:

*Oh, quit your sword, forget your fear,*
*And give me kisses three;*
*If I'm not won ere set of sun,*
*Won never shall I be.*

Surely this was the most hideous creature Childe Wynd had ever seen. And yet, just as surely, he knew it was his sister's voice that came from its awful mouth. Hesitantly he approached the monstrous creature and abruptly brushed its head with his lips. Once, twice, thrice he kissed the Loathsome Dragon. With a hiss and a roar the Loathsome Dragon collapsed to the ground revealing fair Margaret within its heart. Enfolding her in his cloak, Childe Wynd drew his sister forth.

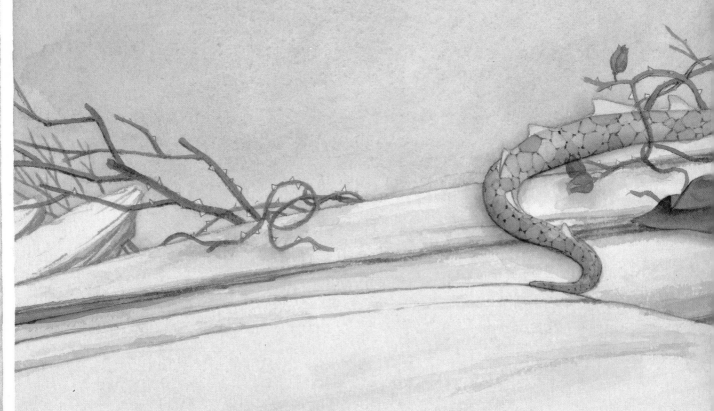

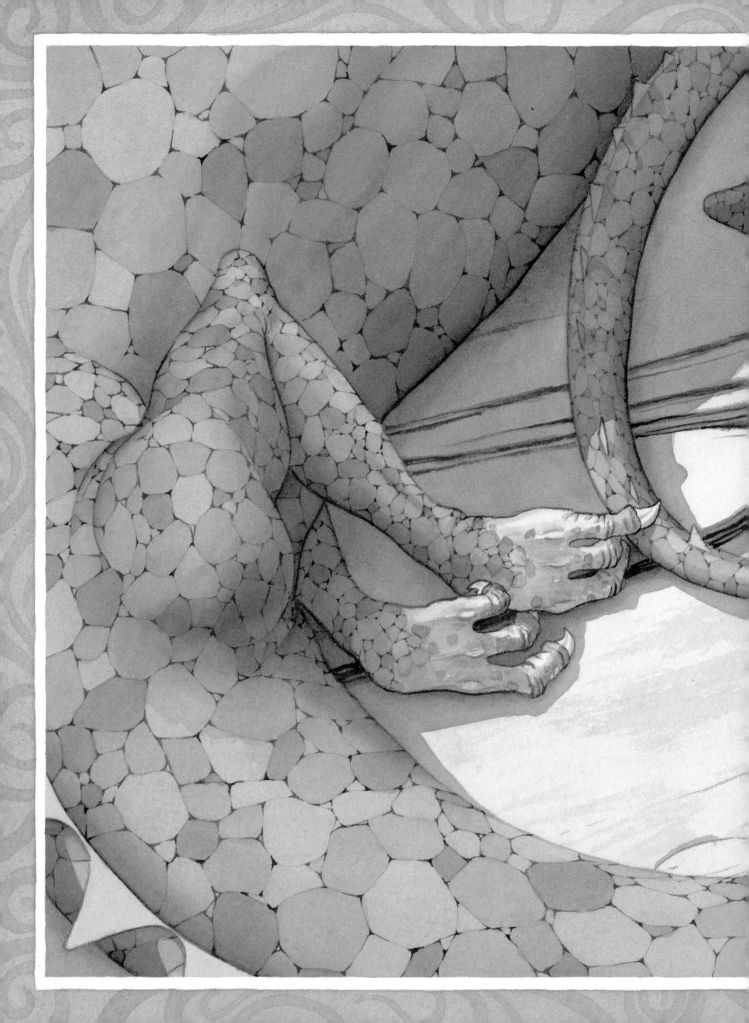

Together, Childe Wynd and Margaret returned to the castle. The Queen stared in shock as they entered the main hall. Childe Wynd drew forth a twig of the rowan tree. A single touch and the Queen slowly shriveled into a Loathsome Toad. It croaked and it hissed and it hopped away down the castle steps.

From that day on, free from enchantment, and with Childe Wynd and Margaret at his side, the King ruled his kingdom, and all lived happily ever after. But to this very day, the Loathsome Toad can still be seen haunting the grounds of Bamborough Castle, croaking in dismay when it sees itself.